Celebrating Chinese Festivals

Celebrating Chinese Festivals

A Collection of Holiday Tales, Poems and Activities

By Sanmu Tang

Better Link Press

This book is edited and designed by the Editorial Committee of *Cultural China* series

Managing Directors: Wang Youbu, Xu Naiqing
Editorial Director: Wu Ying
Editors: Yang Xiaohe, Ginley Regencia

Story and Illustrations: Sanmu Tang
Translation: Yijin Wert

ISBN: 978-1-60220-961-9

Address any comments about *Celebrating Chinese Festivals* to:

Better Link Press
99 Park Ave
New York, NY 10016
USA

or

Shanghai Press and Publishing Development Company
F 7 Donghu Road, Shanghai, China (200031)
Email: comments_betterlinkpress@hotmail.com

Printed in China by Shenzhen Donnelley Printing Co., Ltd.

1 3 5 7 9 10 8 6 4 2

Contents

The Chinese New Year is coming soon! The beautifully decorated streets are full of people. Children are playing drums, performing the lion dance and setting off firecrackers.

6

"Grandpa, why do we celebrate the Chinese New Year?" Little Mei asks.

Her grandpa starts to tell her a touching fairy tale.

9

Long long ago, on the last day of a year, a monster called Xi always came to the human world to cause chaos.

Nian, the grandson of Shennong, came to rescue mankind from Xi.

Nian waved a piece of red ribbon in front of Xi making Xi so dizzy that he lost his balance. Then Nian fed Xi some sticky rice cakes which glued his mouth shut and Xi could no longer bite people.

Finally, Nian set off some firecrackers on Xi's back. Xi was so frightened that he quickly ran away. He did not dare to return to the human world ever again.

12

In memory of Nian, people called the first day of the year
xin nian (New Year), and the last day of the year *chu xi*
(getting rid of Xi).

Now to celebrate the New Year, every house has red 福 (Fortune) banners hanging in the window. Every family makes sticky rice cakes, sets off firecrackers, serves dumplings and sends greetings!

14

"Ooh, these colorful lanterns are so pretty! What's today, Daddy?" Little Mei asks.

"Today is the Lantern Festival. The Lantern Festival falls on the 15th of the first lunar month. This is the first full moon day of the year. Every house lights lanterns and every family eats sweet dumplings," Daddy explains.

"Daddy, why do we light lanterns then?" asks Little Mei.

"Let me tell you the story," Daddy continues.

Long, long ago, a holy bird lost its way and flew toward earth from Heaven. When it landed on earth it was chased and killed by a hunter. This angered the Jade Emperor in Heaven because it was his favorite bird. He wanted to punish mankind, and commanded the God of Fire to send a storm of fire to destroy the earth on the 15th day of the first lunar month.

The Jade Emperor's daughter could not bear to see the people on earth suffer from the fire, so she sneaked down to earth. She made every family light red lanterns around their house, and set off firecrackers on the fifteenth lunar day.

That night, on seeing the earth in red flames and hearing the loud noises from below, the Jade Emperor was extremely satisfied.

20

The plan worked and the people on earth were saved by the Jade Emperor's daughter. From that day on, people celebrate the anniversary on the fifteenth lunar day every year by hanging lanterns around their houses.

21

"The Jade Emperor's daughter was so kind. I am going to make some sweet dumplings for her. Mommy, can you teach me?" Little Mei asks smiling.

 ## How to make sweet dumplings

1. Mix 500g glutinous rice flour with water until it forms a smooth dough.

2. Divide the dough into small portions.

3. Prepare 250g several types of filling (such as red bean paste, black sesame paste).

4. Use your thumb to press a small hole into the dough portions, then fill each with the prepared filling.

5. Fold the edge to seal the dumpling. Lightly roll it into a ball shape using both palms, very gently and delicately.

6. Drop the dumplings into boiling water and cook for 15 minutes.

7. The delicious dumplings are ready to eat!

"Here are all kinds of dumplings. Some are filled with red bean paste, some are filled with black sesame paste, and some are filled with pork or fruit. What kind do you want to try?" Mommy asks.

"I am going to try all of them!" Little Mei is excited to have so many tasty choices.

"After we are done eating, we will go to the Lantern Festival Celebration in the park!"

"Yay! I can't wait to see all the lanterns!"

The park is extremely crowded. People are excitedly gathering around under each lantern and seem to be arguing.

"Daddy, what are they doing?" big sister asks.

"They are trying to solve the lantern riddles. It's actually a lot of fun to solve these brain-teasers. Let's work on a couple of them, too," Daddy says.

"It's a snail!"

No feet, no hands, but walks with his house on his back.

(Guess an animal)

A bucket of gold and a bucket of silver. It won't be closed once it's opened.

(Guess a type of food)

"I wish we could celebrate the Lantern Festival every day," Little Mei says happily.

"I know! It's an egg!"

27

The Qingming Festival
清明节

"Grandma, why did you prepare so much food today? Will we have guests?" Little Mei wants to know.

"Today is the Qingming Festival. It is the time for us to pay respect to our deceased family members with wine and food," Grandmother explains.

29

"What's that green pastry?" asks Little Mei.

"This is a type of sweet green rice ball specially made for the Qingming Festival. Let me show you how to make it," Mommy offers.

How to make sweet green rice balls

1. Place cut mugwort leaves in a blender, mix in a little water and puree into a green juice.

2. Place mugwort juice into a pot, add a little salt and bring to a boil.

3. Mix 500g glutinous rice flour with 200g hot green juice until it forms a smooth dough.

4. Divide the dough into small portions of the same size. Prepare 250g red bean filling by forming smaller balls from red bean paste.

5. Using your thumb, press a small hole into the dough sections and fill with red bean paste balls. Fold the edge to seal the dumpling and lightly roll into a ball. Spray a steamer pot with cooking oil or line it with a layer of bamboo leaf before placing rice balls inside. Steam the rice balls for about 20 minutes until they are fully cooked.

"They're ready! And it does smell like spring is coming."

31

"Grandpa, today I learned a new ancient Chinese poem at school. Do you want to hear it?"

Qingming Festival

Heavy rain drizzles endlessly like tears on the Qingming Day,
The heartbroken mourners are dragging themselves on the road,
May I ask where there's a tavern to drown my sorrows?
The shepherd boy points to a village of the apricot flowers in the distance.

"Good Job! *Qingming Festival* is a poem written over a thousand years ago by Du Mu (803 – 853), a great poet of the Tang Dynasty. The poem describes a lonely man mourning for his loved ones on a rainy Qingming Festival day."

The Dragon Boat Festival
瑞午节

Early in the morning, Daddy hangs some herbs on the front door, and Grandma puts a scented bag over Little Mei's neck. She says this scented bag will keep the evil spirits away.

Mommy brings back some bamboo leaves from the market. She is also soaking plenty of sticky rice in a tub.

"Grandma, is today a special holiday?"

"Yes, today is the 5th day of the 5th lunar month. It is called the Dragon Boat Festival. Mommy is going to make *zongzi*, a special kind of rice packet for this holiday. Let's go and help her."

Making *zongzi* (rice packet)

1. Soak 500g sticky rice in the water until it gets soft.

2. Wash 250g bamboo leaves and soak them in the water to keep them fresh.

3. Prepare 250g fillings such as red dates, pork, red bean paste and red date paste.

4. Fold two bamboo leaves together to form a cone shape. Fill the cone with the sticky rice and fillings, then fold the end of the bamboo leaves over the filling to form a package.

5. Using twine, tie the rice packet tightly.

6. Place the *zongzi* in a large pot cover with water and bring to a boil. Reduce the heat and cook on low heat for five to six hours.

Little Mei enjoys the rice packet so much. She decides to share some with Grandpa. "He will surely tell me the story behind them." Little Mei says to herself.

Over two thousand years ago, in the state of Chu, lived a poet named Qu Yuan. He discovered that the neighboring state of Qin was planning to invade the state of Chu.

Qu Yuan warned the king of the attack. The king not only ignored the warning, but also banished Qu Yuan from his own state.

Several years later, when he heard the news that his state had been conquered by the state of Qin, Qu Yuan lost the will to live. He drowned himself in the Miluo River on the 5th day of the 5th lunar month.

Upon hearing the news of his death, people went out in their boats to look for Qu Yuan's corpse. The villagers threw rice packets into the river to protect Qu Yuan's body from being eaten by the creatures in the river.

That's why people make *zongzi* for the Dragon Boat Festival.

"Let's go! The dragon boat race is starting soon," big
brother shouted excitedly.
Along the river, the drums roar asthe many
colorful dragon boats speed to the
finish line. What a thrilling day!

42

On a fine late summer night, Little Mei and her mother are watching the stars in their backyard.

"Look, Mommy! That looks like a bridge made of stars!"

"That's called the Milky Way. The star on one side of the Milky Way is called Vega and the star on the other side of the Milky Way is called Altair. These names are beautiful, aren't they? There is a lovely fairy tale about these two stars."

Long long ago, a young cowherd named Niu Lang saw nine fairies bathing in the river while he was walking through the forest. He quickly hid behind a tree. The cowherd was so dazzled by the beauty of a young fairy, he became spellbound.

Suddenly his ox began to talk to him, "She is the Weaving Fairy, Zhi Nü, from Heaven. If you take away her colorful dress, she will become your wife." The young cowherd did what his ox said.

At noon, all the other fairies flew back home. Zhi Nü stayed since she could not find her dress. The young cowherd came out from behind the tree and asked Zhi Nü to be his wife. She observed that the young cowherd was an honest and hardworking man. She shyly accepted his marriage proposal.

Two years later, the happy couple were parents to a son and a daughter.

When the Queen of Heaven found her daughter living on earth and married to a cowherd, she became furious.

On the 7th day of the 7th lunar month, she commanded her army to bring Zhi Nü back to Heaven. Niu Lang was extremely worried that his wife was gone. With the help of his ox, he put his two children in baskets and carried them off to Heaven to find Zhi Nü. Niu Lang was about to reach his wife when the Queen showed up, took out her hairpin and marked a line between the two. Instantly, the line became a huge silver river that kept the lovers apart.

The heartbroken Weaving Fairy lived on one side of the river while the cowherd lived on the opposite side with their son and daughter.

Deeply touched by the unhappy outcome of this love story, a flock of magpies decided to help the couple. The birds flew over the river and formed a bridge with their bodies where the family could be reunited.

After seeing their reunion, the Queen of Heaven showed a little mercy, allowing Niu Lang and Zhi Nü to reunite once a year on the 7th day of 7th lunar month.

53

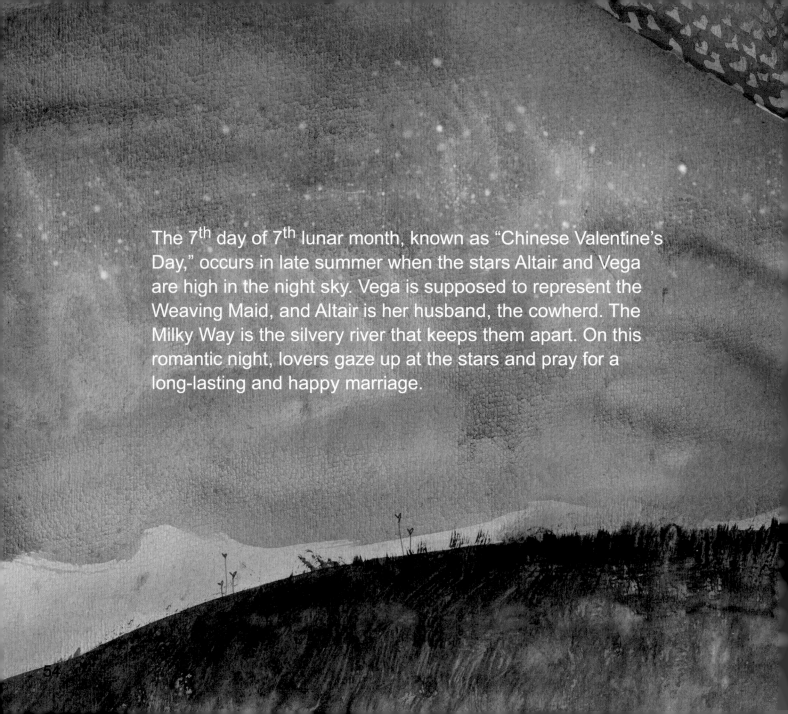

The 7th day of 7th lunar month, known as "Chinese Valentine's Day," occurs in late summer when the stars Altair and Vega are high in the night sky. Vega is supposed to represent the Weaving Maid, and Altair is her husband, the cowherd. The Milky Way is the silvery river that keeps them apart. On this romantic night, lovers gaze up at the stars and pray for a long-lasting and happy marriage.

The Mid-Autumn Festival 中秋节

One day in early fall, Little Mei's Uncle, Aunt and cousin Maomao come to visit her grandparents. They bring some moon cakes with them.

Little Mei grabs Maomao's hand and is very excited to see him. "What kind of holiday is today, Uncle?" asks Little Mei.

56

"Today is the 15th day of the 8th lunar month, called the Mid-Autumn Festival. Tonight the moon will be completely full and bright. It's the time for family reunions. That's why the Mid-Autumn Festival is also called the Family Reunion Festival," Uncle explains.

Long long ago, there were ten suns in the sky burning the earth and scorching the plants. The powerful archer Houyi shot down nine of them to save the people on earth from starvation. The Heavenly Emperor rewarded his heroic deed by giving him a pill that would make Houyi immortal.

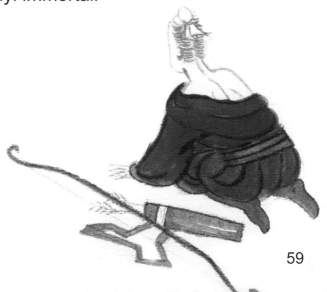

One day, Houyi took his students to an archery practice. One of his students named Pang Meng pretended to be sick and stayed behind. After Houyi left, Pang Meng sneaked into Houyi's house and demanded the immortal pill from Chang'e, Houyi's wife. Chang'e swallowed the pill a second before Pang Meng could grab it.

Suddenly, her body became light, lighter than air. She began to rise, higher and higher towards Heaven, and couldn't get back to earth. As she got close to the moon, she decided to stop and live there as it was still close to earth.

When Houyi came home that night, he missed Chang'e so much that he called and called her name while searching the sky. Suddenly, he saw a figure moving on the moon. It was Chang'e. Houyi set a table out in the yard and put fruits and desserts on the table, gazing at the bright moon, thinking about how could be reunited with his wife.

That was the start of the moon-gazing custom now followed on the Mid-Autumn Festival day.

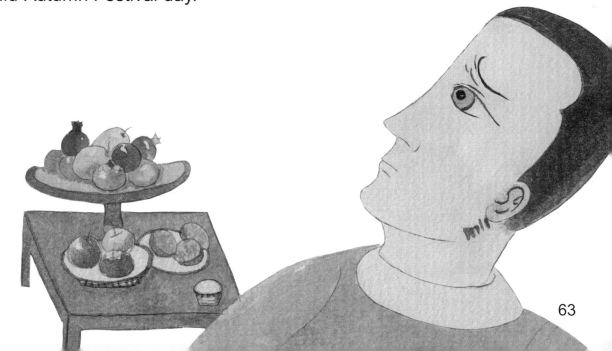

"Little Mei, Maomao, come and help me to make the moon cakes," Grandma says.

Making moon cakes

1. Mix 500g flour with 375g sugar, 7.5g baking soda and 140g oil until it forms a smooth dough.

2. Divide the dough into small sections of the same size and roll out each piece into a pancake.

3. Prepare 4kg red bean paste. Shape red bean paste into small balls. Place the filling in the center of the pancake and gather the edges to enclose the filling. Pinch to seal and create a packet.

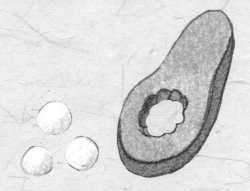

4. Lightly flour the mold and place the filled packet in the mold, gently pressing to fit.

5. Flatten the packet with the palm of your hand, pressing firmly. Then shake the mold to tip out the shaped cake.

6. Brush the moon cakes with beaten egg yolk before putting them into the oven.

7. Bake 20 minutes at 350 degrees and they are ready to eat!

In the bright light of the full moon, Little Mei's family enjoyed a beautiful reunion.

67

The Double Ninth Festival
重阳节

68

It is a beautiful autumn day. Little Mei's family has gone hiking in the mountains to enjoy the blooming chrysanthemums along the trail.

"Mom and Dad, Happy Holiday!" Little Mei's Daddy says to her grandparents.

"Daddy, why didn't you wish me a happy holiday?" Little Mei asks.

"Today is the 9th day of the 9th lunar month, the Double Ninth Festival, also called Chongyang Festival," Grandpa explains, "double nine means health and longevity. This festival honors elderly people like grandma and grandpa."

"Oh, now I understand. I wish Grandpa and Grandma a healthy and long life!"

"Come on, let's read a poem about the Double Ninth Festival," Grandpa says.

Missing My Shandong Brothers on Double Ninth Day

by Wang Wei

A lonely stranger in a foreign land,
Longing to be home for the holidays.
Thinking of my brothers climbing the
mountains on Chongyang Day,
They are wearing dogwood, and I am
not there.

Little Mei loves everything about the festivals: the touching stories, the tasty foods, the beautiful poems and the happy family gatherings.